This book belongs to:

_____

HURRAY FOR Spring!

by
Patricia Hubbell

illustrated by
Taia Morley

HURRAY FOR Spring!

by
Patricia Hubbell

illustrated by
Taia Morley

NORTHWORD PRESS
Minnetonka, Minnesota

The illustrations were created using watercolor and pencil on cold press watercolor board
The text and display type were set in ITC Leawood, Marker Felt, and Curlz
Composed in the United States of America
Designed by Lois A. Rainwater
Edited by Kristen McCurry

Text © 2005 by Patricia Hubbell
Illustrations © 2005 by Taia Morley

NORTHWORD
Books for Young Readers

11571 K-Tel Drive
Minnetonka, MN 55343
www.tnkidsbooks.com

Library of Congress Cataloging-in-Publication Data: Pending

Printed in Singapore
10 9 8 7 6 5 4 3 2 1

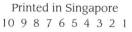

For Jo Gardner,
who loves every season
—P. H.

For Stewart, Franklin, Emma, and Maria
—T. M.

Hurray for spring!
Hurray for spring!

I hop. I skip.
I fly on my swing.

I sing a cloud song.

I dance a leaf dance.

I lie
on my
tummy.

I talk
to the
ants.

I leap a big leap—
jumpity jump!

I watch for a rabbit—
thumpity thump!

Spring tingles my fingers.
It puddles my toes.

It breezes sweet smells
    past my wiggling nose.

I run to my garden.
I plant tiny seeds.

I spy
red-winged
blackbirds
on tall,
springy reeds.

I wriggle with worm.

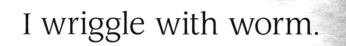

I giggle
with goose.

I peek
between bushes.

I pretend
there's a moose!

I pretend
there's a moose
but he's only
a mouse.

Scampering,
skittering
home
to his
house!

I pick yummy berries.

I lick lemon ice.

Springtime is wildly,
deliciously nice!

I twist and I twirl
like a kite on a string.

I'm swinging

I'm singing

I'm winging

TO SPRING!

PATRICIA HUBBELL has been writing books for children for forty years. Her books have won many honors, including Bank Street College Best Books of the Year; ABA Kids' Pick of the Lists; and the Oppenheim Toy Group Gold Medal. She was also a finalist for the Sequoyah Oklahoma Children's Book Award. Ms. Hubbell began writing poetry when she was in the third grade at Samuel Staples School in Easton, Connecticut, where she still lives today.

TAIA MORLEY has a job most kids dream about: toy designer! She and her husband have a business designing toys and toy packaging. Her career as a picture book illustrator began with *Anna's Table,* written by Eve Bunting. *Hurray for Spring!* is her second book for children. Ms. Morley lives in Stillwater, Minnesota, with her husband and their four children.